To Sharon,

John Bowman

April '98

The Fiddler of the Northern Lights

NATALIE KINSEY-WARNOCK

Illustrated by LESLIE W. BOWMAN

COBBLEHILL BOOKS/Dutton
New York

Text copyright © 1996 by Natalie Kinsey-Warnock
Illustrations copyright © 1996 by Leslie W. Bowman
Library of Congress Cataloging-in-Publication Data
Kinsey-Warnock, Natalie.
The fiddler of the Northern Lights / Natalie Kinsey-Warnock;
illustrated by Leslie W. Bowman.
p.   cm.
Summary: Henry and Grandpa go in search of the fiddler
whose music makes the Northern Lights dance.
ISBN 0-525-65215-9
[1. Fiddlers—Fiction. 2. Auroras—Fiction. 3. Grandfathers—
Fiction.] I. Bowman, Leslie W., ill. II. Title.
PZ7.K6293Fi 1996 [E]—dc20 92-36703 CIP AC

Published in the United States by Cobblehill Books,
an affiliate of Dutton Children's Books,
a division of Penguin Books USA, Inc.,
375 Hudson Street, New York, New York 10014
Designed by Kathleen Westray
Printed in Hong Kong

First edition 10 9 8 7 6 5 4 3 2 1

To Christine.   N.K.W.

To all of us who listen for the sound
of a fiddle when the wind
is just right.   L.W.B.

Far to the north, where wolves howl at the moon, and the stars hang so low and bright it seems you could hop from one to the other, like rocks in a stream, the old folk say that strange and wondrous things sometimes happen.

The Pepin family lived in the north woods along the wild St. Maurice River: Mama, Papa, Armand, Alice, and Henry, who was eight years old. So far, nothing strange or wondrous had happened to Henry, but he knew something might because Grandpa Pepin had told him so.

Henry loved the little cabin and the wild tumbling river that was never out of ear or mind, but most of all he loved when Grandpa Pepin came whistling through the woods to visit. The dark winter days didn't seem so long or lonely when Grandpa Pepin was there, telling his stories of the north woods, legends he'd heard as a boy of the great white owl—*l'hibou blanc*—or the terrible *loup-garou*, who was part man and part wolf.

Some of Grandpa's stories were scary and some were not, but Henry knew them all by heart.

"Did you know that rabbits come out to dance on moonlit nights?" Henry asked Armand when they were ice fishing at the trout holes.

"Who told you that?" Armand said.

"Grandpa Pepin."

"Grandpa Pepin is just making that up," Armand said. "Don't believe any of his stories."

"Do you know what makes the Northern Lights dance?"
Henry asked Mama and Alice when they were carrying
in armloads of wood. Mama and Alice didn't know.

"Magic," said Henry. "And the fiddler."

"What fiddler?" Alice asked.

"When Grandpa was a boy," Henry said, "the old
folk of the village told of a fiddler who lives where the
Northern Lights are born. When he plays his fiddle, he
rouses the lights from sleep, and they dance to his music."

"Oh, Henry," sighed Mama. "That's just one of
Grandpa's stories."

Henry ran all the way to Grandpa's cabin.

"The fiddler is real, isn't he, Grandpa?"

"Why, of course he is," Grandpa said. "But most people never see him."

"I wish I could see him," Henry said. "Couldn't we look for him, sometime, just you and me?"

The next night, Grandpa brought skates he'd made from wood and barrel hoops.

"We're going on an adventure," Grandpa said.

"At night?" Henry asked.

"Sure," said Grandpa. "Night is the best time for adventure, when there's a touch of magic in the air."

"Where are we going, Grandpa?"

"To look for the fiddler," Grandpa said.

Henry and Grandpa strapped the skates to their boots and swooped up the frozen river. The forest and the sky seemed so large and dark, like the mouth of the terrible *loup-garou* ready to swallow them. Henry skated very close to Grandpa.

"Have you ever seen the fiddler?" Henry asked.

"Not yet," said Grandpa. "But maybe we will tonight."

The frozen river was black and smooth like a mirror. Stars glittered in the ice. Henry skated from one to the other, following the stars north.

"The fiddler must be playing," Grandpa said. "See, the Northern Lights are beginning to dance."

The ice shone with the colors of the sky, purple and red and green. Henry and Grandpa skated for miles on that ribbon of sparkling, dancing light.

Henry had never been so far up the river. Once or twice he thought he heard music, but he never saw the fiddler.

Finally, Grandpa stopped.

"I'll just rest a few minutes," Grandpa said.

He sat down and closed his eyes. He looks old, Henry thought.

Henry watched the lights fade, and the river became just a river again, black and smooth. Henry felt tired, too, and a little sad. The fiddler must have been just one of Grandpa's stories, after all.

"We should be getting home," Grandpa said. "They'll be wondering where we are. I'm sorry we didn't find the fiddler."

It was very late before they got back home. Mama gave them both some hot tea and a good scolding.

"You had us worried sick," Mama said. "Where were you?"

"I'm sorry, Angeline," Grandpa said tiredly. "We shouldn't have gone so far up the river."

"We went to find the fiddler," said Henry.

"Oh, Pa," Mama said to Grandpa. "I never want to hear another one of your wild stories."

There was a knock at the door.

"Mercy!" said Mama. "Who else would be out so late on such a cold night?"

A stranger stood in the darkness. His long white beard hung down to his waist and his blue eyes sparkled like stars. Under one arm, he carried a long black box.

"I was out playing tonight, and I was hoping to warm myself by your fire."

Papa told him to come in, and Mama fixed him some hot tea, too.

"What were you playing?" Henry asked.

"My fiddle," the stranger said. "Would you like to hear it?"

Henry and Grandpa smiled at each other.

"We sure would," said Grandpa.

The stranger opened the box and picked up a black fiddle that gleamed in the candlelight.

"We followed the lights up the river," Henry said.
"Can you make them come out again tonight?"
The stranger lifted the fiddle to his chin and began
to play.

The song that poured from the fiddle was as sweet and clear as a mountain stream. As it flowed out into the night, filling up the dark spaces of the sky, the Northern Lights started to dance.

People began to gather around the cabin, neighbors coming from up and down the river. No one on all the wild St. Maurice had ever heard such music, and all who listened knew they'd never hear such music again.

The bright lights leaped from the darkness, spinning and twirling like dancers in their finest gowns.

When the neighbors saw how the lights swayed to the music, they were frightened.

"Don't be afraid," the fiddler said. "I shall play my fiddle and you shall dance all night."

Soon, people filled the cabin to bursting. Chairs and stools were pushed aside to make a dancing floor. The walls rattled with the thumping of feet and the fiddler's music, while the Northern Lights burned overhead.

On and on he played, all through the night,
until they could dance no more.

The music slowed, as sad and lonesome as a wolf howl.
When it stopped, the lights took one last bow and then
they were gone.

"The sun will soon be rising," the fiddler said. "The dance is over and I must be on my way."

He turned toward the north and Grandpa and Henry watched as he disappeared into the woods.

"Off to bed with you," Mama said, hugging Henry.
Then she hugged Grandpa, too.

"Pa, I'll never say another word about your wild
stories," she said.

"You know," Grandpa said. "I didn't believe my wild
stories either—until now," and they all laughed.

Henry never saw the fiddler again. But to this day, when the Northern Lights are sweeping across the sky, there are old folk along the St. Maurice who say that when the wind is just right, you can hear the sound of a fiddle.

As for Grandpa's other stories . . .
Well, Henry still hasn't seen the rabbits dance,
but on moonlit nights, he fills his pockets with
carrots . . . just in case.